FLAT STANLEY

The Haunted House

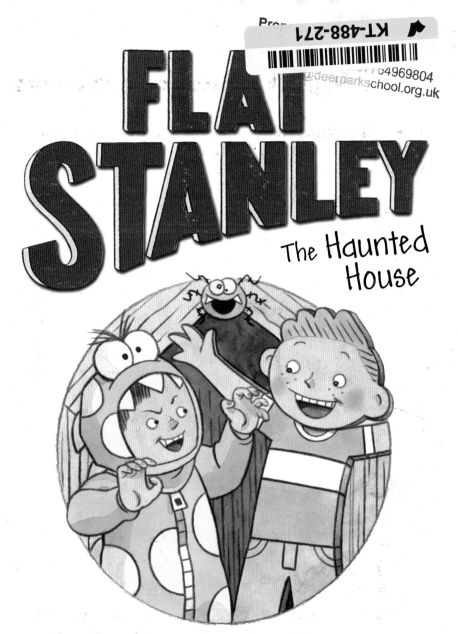

Created by Jeff Brown   Illustrations by Jon Mitchell

Written by Lori Haskins Houran

Reading Ladder

EGMONT

We bring stories to life

Book Band: Turquoise

First published in Great Britain 2011
This Reading Ladder edition published 2016
by Egmont UK Limited
The Yellow Building, 1 Nicholas Road, London W11 4AN
Text and illustrations copyright © 2011 by the Trust u/w/o Richard C. Brown
a/k/a Jeff Brown f/b/o Duncan Brown
ISBN 978 1 4052 8229 1
www.egmont.co.uk
A CIP catalogue record for this title is available from the British Library.
Printed in Singapore
47003/2

Series consultant: Nikki Gamble

MIX
Paper
FSC FSC® C018306

Haunted House

Giant Lollipop

Too Scary

To my wife Jayne, two sons Thomas & Joseph
and Alfie & Marley
Jon Mitchell

Haunted House

Stanley Lambchop lived with his mother,

his father and his little brother, Arthur.

Stanley was four feet tall, about

a foot wide, and half an inch thick.

He had been flat ever since

a bulletin board fell on him.

Mostly Stanley liked being flat.

He was very good at dodge ball

and hide-and-seek.

Hee hee!

Stanley's school was having

a Halloween party.

'Will there be limbo at our party?'

asked Stanley.

He was very good at limbo, too.

'Yes,' said Mrs Lambchop.

'I want to see the haunted house,'

said Arthur. 'I hope it's really scary!'

'Not too scary,' said his mother.

'There will be small children

at the party.'

Mrs Lambchop zipped up

Arthur's monster costume.

She had sewn it herself.

'Perfect,' she said. 'Scary. But not

too scary.'

Stanley put on his costume, too.

He was a blueberry pancake.

'You look good enough to eat,'

Mrs Lambchop said. 'Let's go!'

Arthur and Mrs Lambchop got in the car.

Mr Lambchop tied Stanley to the

roof rack.

Let's go!

'All set, Stanley?' he asked.

'All set,' Stanley answered.

The school gym was full of

pirates and witches and fairies.

'Hey, look!' Arthur said.

'Hay is for horses, Arthur,'

Mrs Lambchop told him.

'I know,' said Arthur. 'Look!'

A horse trotted by.

'Oh,' said Mrs Lambchop. 'Sorry, dear.'

'That's the haunted house!'

Arthur said to Stanley.

They stood in line behind the horse.

'What a clever costume,'

the horse's mother said to Stanley.

'You look as flat as a pancake!'

At last, their turn came.

'Come on,' said Stanley.

The boys stepped inside.

'BOO!' yelled a ghost.

Arthur thought the ghost's trainers

looked like Mr Bart's, the PE teacher.

A werewolf howled. Then it sneezed.

Atchoo!

'Bless you!' said the ghost politely
to the werewolf.

19

'This isn't scary at all!' Stanley said.

'Let's get out of here, Arthur.'

Giant
Lollipop

Outside, Arthur and Stanley

saw a little boy crying.

It was their neighbour, Martin Tibbs.

What's the matter?

'What's wrong?' asked Stanley.

'Did the haunted house scare you?'

'No,' Martin sniffled.

Martin told them that a bully
had stolen his giant lollipop.
'It was my prize for winning
the limbo contest,' he said sadly.

'I missed the limbo contest?

Rats!' said Stanley.

'Where did the mean kid go?'

asked Arthur.

Martin pointed across the gym.

Gulp!

An older boy leaned against the wall.

Next to him was the lollipop.

'That's one big lollipop!' said Arthur.

'That's one big kid,' said Stanley.

Stanley looked at Arthur's costume.

'I have an idea,' he said.

'Make room for me, Arthur!'

Stanley took off his costume

and slipped inside Arthur's.

Then he whispered in Arthur's ear.

'Great plan,' Arthur said.

'Just don't blink!'

Too Scary

Arthur walked over to the big kid.

Stanley didn't blink.

'Give that lollipop back or else,'

Arthur demanded. 'Or else what?' said

the bully.

'I'll tell everyone that you're scared of me,' said Arthur.

The kid stood up tall.

He stepped right in front of

Arthur and Stanley.

Stanley still didn't blink.

'Why should I be scared of you?'

the bully growled.

Grr!

'I'm a two-headed monster,'

Arthur said.

39

The boy pointed to Stanley's face.

'Ha! That head is so fake,' he said.

Then Stanley blinked.

'Fake?' said Stanley. 'Oh, really?'

'AAAAAAHHH!' yelled the bully.

He ran out the gym door,

leaving the lollipop behind.

'YES!' yelled Stanley and Arthur.

They jumped up and down

inside Arthur's costume.

'Ow! My toes!' Arthur yelled.

Martin picked up his lollipop.

'Thanks, guys!' he said.

'Uh-oh,' said Arthur.

Stanley turned around.

Mr and Mrs Lambchop

were standing behind him.

46

'Arthur and Stanley Lambchop,

I saw what you did,'

Mrs Lambchop said sternly.

'That was scary.'

Then Mrs Lambchop smiled.

'TOO scary!'